MW00890169

The Sweetest Rainbow

Cayla Smith

Dedicated to My Berkley

Good morning World,
as we begin to pray.
Be with us God
as we start our day.

As the sun comes up,
it's a brand new day.
"We can't wait to play!"
both the little girls say.

2+1 will equal 3.
They looked around....
Is he talking to me?

"I've picked you two to help me out. I need your help; Can you girls do that?"

With a sweet bundle of joy
for you both to teach
and show her daily
what true love means.

With each passing day
mommy's belly grew and grew.
We couldn't wait
for the date that she was due!!!

OCTOBER

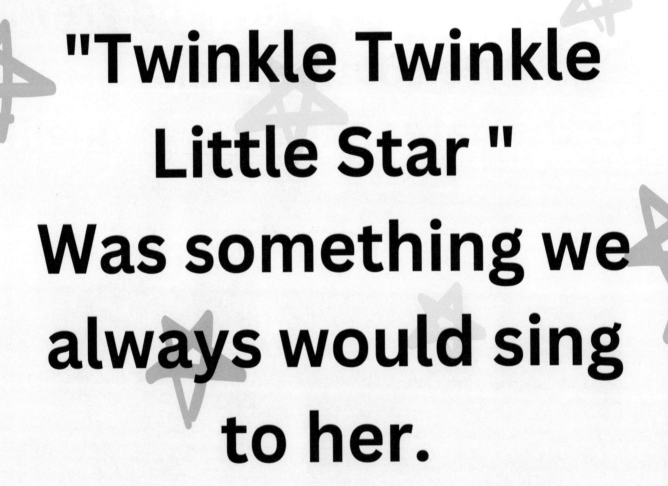

"Twinkle Twinkle
Little Star "
Was something we
always would sing
to her.

Our hearts grew excited
with every minute that passed.
Until one day
God suddenly called her back.

Our minds kept racing
with so many questions.
" Why did God need her back?
Why did this have to happen?"

The sweetest rainbows
seemed to randomly appear;
On the doctor office door and
even talked about on Eeyore.

"It's a Rainbow
kinda day "
That sure was true,
if I must say.

Now with every gorgeous rainbow we spot through out the days...

God's reassuring comfort
let's us know that your okay.

She lets us know,
"Look Momma don't cry ,
I'm right here.
God has me in his arms so
there is nothing to fear ."

The bright colors
that shine through & through
make our day brighter
just to think of you.

Red is for the love
we had from day one
when we learned the
special news
that a blessing was to
come.

Orange is for the excitement
that little minds
could not contain.

Yellow is for the
brightness
that you brought to all our
minds
about the things you girls
would do
now as 3 and not just 2.

Green is for the memories that we made in 4 short months.
From your sweet heart beat to the kicks of your little feet.

Blue is how we feel
with all the tears cried
missing you.
How our hearts are
crushed
and the tears continue to
rush.

Little hearts
don't understand.
Big hearts
have a hard time too.

Purple is for the promise that we will see you again real soon!!!

Together all the colors
make things a brighter
shade of blue.

They remind us of
the sweetest rainbow
and that
will always be
YOU.

So shine bright
Our rainbow baby,
until we see you again one day.

You are such a precious blessing in each & every way!

Made in the USA
Columbia, SC
23 July 2024

38589108R00018